TOBY BELFER
Never Had a Christmas Tree

Gloria Teles Pushker

TOBY BELFER
Never Had a Christmas Tree

Illustrated by Judith Hierstein

PELICAN PUBLISHING COMPANY
Gretna 1994

First printing, September 1991
Second printing, September 1994

*To the Magnificent Seven—Adam, Paul,
Melissa, Ryan, James, Matthew, & Courtney
(whose grandmother's grandmother was really
and truly named Toby Belfer)*

*and to Coleen Salley, who had faith in me and
taught me well*

and to Bluma

Library of Congress Cataloging-in-Publication Data

Pushker, Gloria Teles.
    Toby Belfer never had a Christmas tree / by Gloria Teles
Pushker; illustrated by Judith Hierstein.
        p. cm.
    Summary: Living in a small Louisiana town where hers is the
only Jewish family, Toby Belfer gives a party for her friends in
order to explain Hannukah, including the story of Judah
Maccabee, the significance of the menorah, how to make potato
latkas, and how to play the game of dreydl.
    ISBN 0-88289-855-8
    [1. Hanukkah—Fiction. 2. Jews—Fiction.] I. Hierstein, Judy,
ill. II. Title.
PZ7.P97943To 1991
[E]—dc20   91-14514
                                                                          CIP
                                                                           AC

Printed in Singapore

Published by Pelican Publishing Company, Inc.
1101 Monroe Street, Gretna, Louisiana 70053

It was never at all difficult being the only Jewish family in a small, south Louisiana town. We drove thirty-five miles to the next town in order to attend a small but lovely temple. We celebrated every holiday to the fullest, and our three daughters grew up respecting and being good friends with our Christian neighbors, yet knowing their own culture and traditions and loving their Jewish heritage.

Toby Belfer never had a Christmas tree. She never wondered why. She knew that she was Jewish, and that was reason enough.

Hers was the only Jewish family in the little country town where she lived with her parents and her grandmother. They loved the **Torah** and followed its laws.

Toby lived in a small cottage with a great big yard with lots of flowers and trees, and a swing, and a slide, and a dog.

All the boys and girls in the neighborhood loved to come to Toby's to play. When the weather was sunny they played games in the garden or climbed the trees, but when it was raining they sat on the porch swing and sang songs, and sometimes Mrs. Belfer baked cookies and told them wonderful stories. It was a place where they always had a lot of fun.

It was wintertime, and the children were excited that Christmas was coming soon. They invited Toby to their houses to trim their trees and sing lovely Christmas carols. That was a lot of fun, too, but Toby Belfer never had a Christmas tree herself.

One December night, Toby invited her friends to her house for a party. Before the guests arrived, Mrs. Belfer set the table with her finest tablecloth and dishes.

Meanwhile, Toby and her grandmother were busy in the kitchen peeling and grating potatoes for pancakes they called **latkas**. After that was done, they squeezed the potatoes dry and added a small, grated onion, a little salt and pepper, and two eggs.

That felt mushy!

Some people added two tablespoons of flour, but Grandmother used **matzo meal** instead to firm up the mixture. That was her secret for great-tasting, great-smelling, crisp potato latkas.

When the children arrived, to their delight they saw standing in the living room a tall candle holder made of wood. Mr. Belfer said it was a **menorah**.

He had built it himself by nailing together three pieces of wood in the shape of a *T*. Across the top he glued nine bottle tops, which he painted a gold color. They were used to hold eight long candles, to remember each night of **Hanukkah**, and one extra helper which was called a **shamash**.

At the table, Grandmother Belfer lit the shamash and then lit the single twisted, colored candle that had been placed on the right side in her beautiful old brass menorah.

Toby had her own menorah. It was just the right size for birthday candles. With the shamash she lit the first candle for the first night. The little candle shone brightly.

Grandmother Belfer held up her hands and led the family in three prayers. They all said them together, first in Hebrew and then in English:

"Baruch atah Adonai, Elohenu melech ha'olam, asher kidishanu, bamitzvotov vitzevanu lahadlik ner shel Hanukkah. Amen."

"Blessed art Thou, O Lord our God, King of the universe, who commanded us to kindle the lights of Hanukkah. Amen."

"Baruch atah Adonai, Elohenu melech ha'olam, she-oso nisim la-votenu bayomim ho-hem baz'man haze."

"Blessed art Thou, O Lord our God, King of the universe, who has blessed our fathers and watched over them in the days of old."

"Baruch atah Adonai, Elohenu melech ha'olam shehecheyanu vekeyemanu vehigianu lazman hazeh."

"Blessed art Thou, O Lord our God, King of the universe, who gave us life, sustained us, and brought us to this happy season."

The children gathered around the table for a special treat of latkas. They were delicious with applesauce.

They played a game with a top called **dreidel**. The prize for winning was chocolate money called **gelt**.

They sang Hanukkah songs, and Toby told the exciting
story of how Judah Maccabee and his followers had to fight
the armies of the powerful Syrian king Antiochus to rebuild
the temple in Jerusalem and bring the Jewish people reli-
gious freedom long, long ago.

Antiochus wanted all nations to bow down to his idols,
but the Jews refused. They would bow only to God!

Other nations spent time in arenas and large buildings watching games held in honor of these gods, but the Jews spent their time studying the Torah. This made the king very angry, so he had his army place a statue of Zeus, his favorite idol, in the holy temple in Jerusalem. He had pigs sacrificed on the altar, which was a great insult to the Jews, and he destroyed everything else that was there.

He was so angry with the Jews that he decided that if any person was found reading the holy books or honoring the Sabbath, he would be put to death.

So guess what they did!

When the Jewish boys were studying the Torah and the soldiers of Antiochus came around, the boys pretended to be playing a game of dreidel.

After the fighting stopped, Judah Maccabee and his followers began to clean and rebuild the temple, and they once more made it a place of beauty—a place to worship God in peace. They were very upset to find that only one little jar of sacred oil remained to relight the **Ner Tamid**, the eternal light—only enough to last one night. Jewish law says that the flame must always be burning over the holy ark in the temple.

A GREAT MIRACLE HAPPENED THERE!

That little jar of oil burned for eight nights until new oil could be prepared, giving all the world THE FESTIVAL OF LIGHTS!

So you see, that is why at Hanukkah the candles are lit to remember those days.

> On the first night of Hanukkah
> We light one glowing light
> To shine in the window and
> Brighten up the night.
>
> Two candles for the second night
> As in days of old
> Three for the third night
> Shimmering like gold.
>
> Four candles for the fourth night
> Until it's eight for eight
> Our friends come to us each night
> To help us celebrate.

Toby gave everyone a present, and all the boys and girls were invited to come back every night for the eight nights of Hanukkah. It was wonderful.

The children of that little country town learned a lot about Jewish traditions. They also learned how nice it could be to have friends who could teach them new things about their different cultures. Everyone was very happy that TOBY BELFER NEVER HAD A CHRISTMAS TREE....

Happy Hanukkah from Toby Belfer.

GRANDMOTHER'S RECIPE
FOR POTATO LATKAS

2 pounds of potatoes, peeled and finely grated
1 small onion, grated (optional)
2 eggs, well beaten
2 tablespoons of flour or matzo meal
salt and pepper to taste
vegetable oil for frying
   serves 8

Squeeze the grated potatoes to get the last of the water out of them. Place in a bowl. Mix in eggs, one grated onion (optional), flour or matzo meal, and seasonings. Heat about 1/2 inch of oil in a heavy frying pan and fry large spoonsful of the mixture until brown and crisp on both sides. Drain on absorbent paper. Serve hot with applesauce.

RULES OF THE GAME OF DREIDEL

Any number of children or adults can participate.

1. Everyone starts with the same amount of gelt, or nuts if you prefer.
2. To begin, everyone puts one piece of gelt or one nut into the "kitty."
3. Each takes a turn to spin the dreidel.
4. Based on what the dreidel says when it falls, the players then take out, put in, or do nothing.

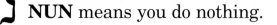 **NUN** means you do nothing.

GIMMEL means you take everything and spin again.

HAY means you take half of what is in the "kitty."

SHIN means you must add a piece of gelt or a nut.

The object of the game is for someone to win all the nuts or the gelt.

NOTE: A dreidel is a four-sided top which comes in all sizes and colors and which may be purchased at any temple gift shop.

HOW TO BUILD A BIG MENORAH

You will need:

2 two-by-fours that are each four feet long

1 piece of wood that is 1" X 12" X 12"

9 bottle tops from 2-liter containers to use as candle holders

gold paint

very strong nails for the wood

very strong glue for the candle holders

Nail the two four-foot boards together in the shape of a *T*. Then nail the bottom of the *T* to the 12" square piece of wood to form the base. Glue bottle tops to top board, putting four on each side and one in the middle for the shamash. Paint entire menorah gold.

DO NOT LIGHT THESE CANDLES. THIS IS ONLY FOR SHOW.